LOVE IS MY FAVORITE THING

Emma Chichester Clark

SCHOLASTIC INC.

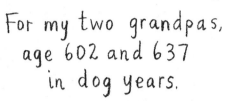

For my two grandpas,
age 602 and 637
in dog years.

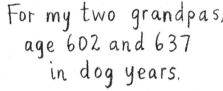

Also published in Great Britain by Random House Children's Publishers UK in 2015

No part of this publication may be reproduced, stored in a retrieval system, or transmitted
in any form or by any means, electronic, mechanical, photocopying, recording,
or otherwise, without written permission of the publisher. For information regarding
permission, write to Nancy Paulsen Books, an imprint of Penguin Young Readers Group,
a division of Penguin Random House LLC, 375 Hudson Street, New York, NY 10014.

ISBN 978-1-338-16629-3

12 11 10 9 8 7 6 5 4 3 2   17 18 19 20 21 22

Printed in the U.S.A.   40

First Scholastic printing, January 2017

The art was done in watercolor and colored pencil.

I AM PLUM,
but I love being called Plummie.

And **LOVE** is my favorite thing.

I love all kinds
of weather,
especially wind.

(But I don't
really love rain.)

I love snow,

and I love sun.

I love my bear

and my bed.

I love treats

and
catching.

I love sticks
SO much,

but LOVE IS MY VERY FAVORITE THING!

I love Sam and Gracie, who live next door.

I love it when they come over to play at my house.

And I love Emma and Rupert.
They are my family.
I love it when they say,
"You are a very good girl, Plummie!"
Then, I feel loved all over.

I love the park and my friends.
I love the grass and the trees.
I love it when Emma says, "Good girl, Plummie!"
when I go, as if it's so, so clever.

I know it means she loves me,
and LOVE is my favorite thing.

But this morning, **EVERYTHING** went wrong.

When Emma said "Don't go in the pond, Plummie!" I wasn't listening.

I heard Rocket say, "Come on, Plum! Come on!"

No! Plum!

And I just couldn't help it. I really couldn't.

PLUM! Come back!

Water is one of my other favorite things! I love it! LOVE it!

PLUM! COME HERE, AT ONCE!

"Isn't this great?" said Rocket. And it was. It really was . . .

...until
Emma arrived.
"BAD GIRL!"
she shouted.

And I knew I'd made
a **BIG** mistake.
She marched me home.

Sam and Gracie
heard what I'd done.
"Oh, Plum!" said Gracie.
"Oh, Plum!" said Sam.
Will they still love me?

I ran to find them
a present but . . .

. . . I only found a cushion.
When Gracie tried
to take it . . .

. . . I just couldn't help it!
I really couldn't. Tug-of-war
is my **favorite** game!

I love it! I LOVE it!
"No! Plum!" cried Gracie.

"No! No, PLUM!" cried Sam.
They were pulling and
I was pulling . . .

. . . then I was flying
and SUDDENLY . . .

"PLUM!" shouted Emma.

"VERY BAD GIRL!" she said.

"TIME-OUT FOR YOU!"
said Emma, and I realized
I'd made a big mistake.
"Oh, Plum!" said Gracie.
"Oh, Plum!" said Sam.

Will any of them
still love me?

That afternoon, we all went to the park.
It was sunny and bright, and everywhere I looked,
I saw toddlers with ice cream.
"Plummie," said Emma, "that's NOT for you!"

But I really
love ice cream.

I know what
it tastes like
and I love it!

Come
on, Plum!

I just
LOVE it!

And toddlers are **always** dropping things . . .

. . . they drop things **right** in front of me . . .

. . . and I just couldn't help it . . . I really couldn't . . . so I grabbed it!

"PLUM!" cried Emma.
Then everyone was running
and everyone was chasing!

I ran to my house and waited.
I knew that I'd made
THE MOST ABSOLUTELY
AWFUL MISTAKE!

"Oh, Plum!" said Gracie.

"Oh, Plum!"
said Sam.

"Oh, Plum!"
said Emma.

"What a NAUGHTY girl!"
said Emma.

She marched me downstairs and sent me to my bed.

I was so happy
when they came
and opened
the door.

"Well, Plum," said Rupert.
"Are you sorry?"

And I was. I really was.
I'd do **ANYTHING!**
as long as they
still love me.

"BUT DO YOU STILL
LOVE ME?

DO YOU STILL
LOVE ME?"

"Oh, Plummie!" said Emma.
"Oh, Plummie!" said Rupert.
"We do love you! But—you've got to try
to behave and do as you're told, and
BE A GOOD GIRL!
Can you do that?" he asked.

I can do that,
I REALLY CAN TRY!

So I do try to behave.
I don't always remember—
I wish that I could.
I still make mistakes, but I know they love me.
They do! They really do!

AND THAT'S WHY
LOVE IS MY FAVORITE THING!